DISNEY'S
WINNIE THE POOH'S
STORIES FOR CHRISTMAS

By Bruce Talkington
Illustrated by John Kurtz

DISNEY
PRESS

NEW YORK

Contents

I love the night before Christmas," exclaimed Christopher Robin as he and Pooh, bundled warmly in bright-colored mufflers and black, shiny boots, walked side by side through the snow-covered Hundred-Acre Wood. "Don't you, Pooh Bear?"

"Why yes," responded Pooh thoughtfully, "now that you mention it, I do." Then, like a balloon blocking the sun, the bear's brow furrowed into a frown. "But . . . ," he murmured.

"But *what*, Pooh?" Christopher Robin wanted to know.

"Isn't *every* night a night before one Christmas or another?" he asked, rubbing his suddenly muddled head. "Sort of?"

"Well," answered a surprised Christopher Robin, "that is true, Pooh Bear. Sort of."

Christopher Robin stopped walking and looked down at Pooh, who also stopped walking and looked up at Christopher Robin, leaning so far back to see his friend's face above him that he almost sat down in the snow.

"But I'm talking about Christmas *Eve*," explained Christopher Robin carefully, "and about all the things that happen on that night that make it so very special."

"Ah," exclaimed Pooh, finally understanding. And as they continued their walk, the bear of little brain but bountiful appetite considered the things he loved about this night. And a certain Christmas Eve popped out of his memory that was very special because he had had the opportunity to do more of the thing that made *every* night, for Pooh Bear, a little bit of the night before Christmas.

His tummy remembered, too, and rumbled its recollection of . . .

The Bite Before Christmas

'Twas the night before Christmas
With snow soft and new,
Not a creature was stirring
Except Winnie the Pooh!

The bear of little brain was dressed warmly in his favorite flannel nightshirt with its matching cap (topped by a very snazzy red tassel) and was tucked cozily into bed with quilts, blankets, and sheets pulled snugly up under his chin.

But his eyes were wide open and staring (because that's what wide-open eyes do), and sleep was the last thing on his mind.

"Oh bother," he sighed. And, as if to emphasize his restlessness, he immediately followed it with "Oh BOTHER, bother!"

Surprisingly, it wasn't the imminent arrival of Christmas, the tingling anticipation of tomorrow morning's full stocking dangling from the mantel, or the beribboned presents piled under the tree, that was keeping the bear awake.

No, what was bouncing about in the fluff of Pooh's head was the same thing that was bouncing about it at this particular time *every* night.

"A small smackeral of something sweet," smiled Pooh dreamily, smacking his lips.

Pooh worked very hard at making sure his honey and his day ran out at the same time. But in the middle of the night, *every* night, like some sort of internal alarm clock, Pooh Bear's tummy would begin to rumble and growl until the entire bed appeared to be buzzing and vibrating. He tried his best not to notice, knowing that daytime was for eating and nighttime was for sleeping, but this was what Pooh called the hungry part of the night, and there was simply no ignoring it if you were a bear to whom the world was a place where it was *always* time for breakfast!

"And a very nice sort of world it is, too," Pooh chuckled as he sat up in bed.

Tossing back his covers, Pooh slid out from beneath the bedclothes and dropped feetfirst into the slippers waiting patiently by the bed. Thumpety-thump, thumpety-thump, the slippers echoed on the hard wooden floors as the bear headed for his favorite part of his house—his favorite part of any house, for that matter—the kitchen!

There was no need to light a candle or a lamp because a full moon gleamed across the new snow blanketing the wood, making night appear as bright as day!

Pooh's face fell, however, at the sight that greeted him upon arriving in the kitchen. It was a most unhappy collection of dirty dishes, soiled silverware, and spotted saucepans. He'd forgotten to remember the mess he'd made preparing, tasting, baking, tasting, tasting again, and packing all the Christmas treats he'd cooked for his friends, treats that they

would allow him to help eat after all the presents were unwrapped tomorrow. In the meantime, however, his kitchen was turned inside out and his pantry was decidedly and undeniably as empty as his stomach.

"Oh my goodness gracious," sighed Pooh as his tummy emitted such a growl that it set the dishes, piled haphazardly into precarious towers, rattling in sympathy. "If this is a dream, I'd like to wake up right now, if that's quite all right with whoever is in charge of dreaming, of course."

He closed his eyes for a moment to let the dream disappear. But when he squinted one eye open for a peek and saw that nothing had changed from its former untidiness, he knew a bad dream wasn't the problem.

Pooh's head was quite willing to accept this great

disappointment and return quietly to bed, but his middle was not being nearly so reasonable. It growled and hummed and gurgled, kicking up such a fuss that Pooh could almost see his tummy churning underneath his nightshirt.

"No doubt about it," murmured Pooh, "someone's going to have to do something about this. And since Pooh Bear, which is me, is the only someone about, I suppose I . . . I mean, him . . . er, me . . . WE are going to be the one . . . two . . . to do it!" He scrunched his forehead into a frown and scratched his ear fiercely. He was very glad there was only one of him because counting any higher was not something he did very well. "But what are we . . . am I . . . to do?"

All at once, an idea occurred so quickly that Pooh almost didn't realize what it was! Ideas not being something he was very used to having occur at *any* time, it was especially disconcerting to have one happen along when he truly needed

it! It was so sudden, in fact, and so unexpected, that Pooh almost forgot it even while it was taking place. The only thing that saved it from drifting away to where most of Pooh's ideas disappeared was the simple fact that it involved food. Food was something Pooh's tummy was simply not going to allow him to forget, no matter how stuffed with fluff a bear's *head* happened to be.

What Pooh remembered was a certain snack.

When Christmas Eve arrived, *everyone* was anxious that Santa not go hungry during his long night's work. Rabbit always set out a steaming bowl of his flavorful vegetable stew. Piglet, who could never make up his mind as to what Santa might find the most appetizing, provided a mug of hot cocoa and a list of what was to be found in his very small but well-stocked pantry, along with an invitation for Santa to help himself!

Pooh thought a snack was a good idea at any time, even when it wasn't for him. So every Christmas Eve, he placed a plateful of homemade gingerbread snowmen and a big glass of frosty milk on the fireplace hearth in expectation of Santa's need for a rest after packing the sackful of mostly edible presents Pooh was always in hopes of receiving all the way from the North Pole!

Thumpety-thump, thumpety-thump, thumpety-THUMP! Pooh scurried toward the living room, licking his lips in anticipation. He was certain that Santa wouldn't begrudge him one little cookie—perhaps two—and a small sip of cold milk.

In less time than it takes to eat a plate of cookies and empty a glass of milk (which is hardly any time at all in Pooh's house), Pooh was sprawled in his favorite armchair, his feet perched comfortably upon the ottoman, an empty glass of

milk in one hand, half of the last gingerbread snowman cookie in the other, and a frothy milk mustache under his nose!

Needless to say, Pooh was at this moment quite cozy, and his tummy was, temporarily at least, quite satisfied. He leaned his head against the back of the chair and let his mind consider one of the truly important questions in the life of a bear of little brain.

"Why is it," Pooh asked himself while stifling a very insistent yawn, "that we have TWO hands for stuffing honey, but only ONE mouth to stuff?"

The only answer that came to him was the prodigious yawn that simply refused stifling.

The next thing the bear knew, he was being shaken gently awake by a cold hand. He lifted his sleepy eyelids, and his eyes immediately opened with an amazed *POP* at what they saw! It was Santa Claus, leaning over Pooh and smiling happily into his face!

"Oh!" gasped Pooh, because "oh!" is what is usually gasped when a surprise takes place.

"Pooh Bear!" exclaimed Santa, ceasing to shake him. "I certainly am glad to see you! Ho-ho-ho!"

"You are?" responded the bear, more than a bit disconcerted because that's exactly what he was going to say to Santa—except for the ho-ho-ho part, of course.

"Oh my goodness, yes," sighed Santa in what seemed to be great relief. "In fact, I had just decided my problem was quite important enough to wake you."

Santa placed his hand on Pooh's shoulder. "I need your help," he announced solemnly.

Pooh's ears instantly pricked up to listen because he knew what needing help was all about. But, he thought to himself, how can I possibly help Santa Claus?

"It's all these wonderful snacks," answered Santa as if Pooh had asked the question aloud. "Everyone has thoughtfully left me goodies, goodies, and more goodies to refresh me on my rounds. Well, I still have a very long way to go, and . . . ," he sighed heavily, ". . . I'm FULL!"

Pooh blinked his eyes rapidly in surprise. Being FULL was a feeling with which he was not at all familiar. This was quite all right with him, however, because he'd always found the "doing" of a thing much more exciting than the "having done" part, especially when what one was doing was eating, whether breakfast or lunch or dinner or any small (or large) sort of smackeral in between!

"And," Santa continued, "it's very important not to hurt anyone's feelings." He looked Pooh Bear in the eye. "Do you suppose you and your appetite could come along with me tonight and deal with some of this food?"

A happy smile spread itself over Pooh's face, and his tummy agreed with a particularly enthusiastic rumble.

Santa smiled back, his eyes twinkling merrily.

"Ho-ho-HO!" Santa laughed. "That sounds like a YES to me!"

The next thing Pooh knew, he was seated next to Santa in the toy-laden sleigh, wearing his slippers, nightshirt, and

cap (still topped with its snazzy red tassel) and was snuggled comfortably beneath a fuzzy blanket.

"Ready?" inquired Santa with a grin.

Pooh nodded nervously. "I suppose I am."

A slight flick of Santa's wrists sent the reindeer soaring into the air in an explosion of chiming sleigh bells.

Within a very short time Pooh was eating yam cake and root beer in front of the sleeping Gopher's fire as Santa filled the stocking dangling from the mantel.

At Tigger's, while the sounds of feline snoring resounded from the bedroom, Santa went about his business, and Pooh dined on oatmeal cookies striped with rows of chocolate chips.

The snack at Kanga and Roo's house consisted of a great

many very small peanut butter cookies and a dainty cup of lemon tea.

By the time they left Eeyore's house and the remnants of his bowlful of brownies, flying off into the world beyond the Hundred-Acre Wood, Pooh Bear was losing track of what was being eaten where!

The night became a blur of whirling flights and good things to eat. One moment Santa was whizzing past the moon, the next Pooh was seated comfortably in one strange living room or another slurping noodles in China, sipping hot onion soup afloat with melted cheese in France, devouring Danish pastries in Denmark, and licking luscious ice cream in Iceland!

Soon, even the bottomless Pooh was unable to

distinguish one country from another because all he knew was that he was truly full at last and couldn't possibly eat another bite. This might have made anyone else sad, but Pooh knew, as certainly as bees meant honey and Christmas meant Santa Claus, that tomorrow morning the arrival of breakfast would coincide with his being ready to eat it. He was, however, a bit uneasy about whether or not there would be anything at home to serve at the anticipated breakfast.

"Don't worry, Pooh," laughed Santa as he clapped the bear on the back, "we won't let any of this food go to waste!"

Thereafter, as a bag was emptied of toys it was refilled with all sorts of savories, sweets, stews, soups, and sauces!

As this went on and on, Pooh cuddled comfortably beneath his blanket with a soft smile on his face and a warm feeling in his middle. The swoops and twirls of the flying sleigh, the wind rushing against his closed eyes, the ho-ho-ho-ing from Santa as he shouted encouragement to his reindeer blended together and drifted away until it all seemed like such a . . . DREAM?

Pooh sat up, suddenly wide awake, only to discover himself in his own bed with a sparkling Christmas morning shining through the windows into his bedroom. He didn't remember going to bed, but, as Tigger would tease him, not 'memberin' is one o' the things Pooh Bears do best!

"It was all a dream," he decided. "And a very nice one, at that!"

Then he smiled and patted his middle. "Such a good dream that even my tummy was fooled into thinking it's not hungry."

His tummy responded with a low rumble.

"Well," Pooh chuckled, "not VERY hungry."

Immediately, Winnie the Pooh jumped out of bed and, ignoring his slippers, went slipping and sliding across the polished wooden floors into his kitchen. There he found not a single dish or pot or saucepan dirty or out of place! And his pantry! Oh, his pantry! It was crammed from top to bottom with food from all over the world.

"Oh my!" breathed Pooh wonderingly. "Where did all this

come from?" Then the tickle of recollection at the back of his mind burst forth into a giggle of remembering his wish list to Santa. It had included requests for as many mouthwatering delicacies as he could think of, and there they all were filling his pantry and, of course, making his mouth water!

"It's better than a dream," sighed Pooh. "Unless, of course, it *is* a dream," he added with a puzzled frown.

"But whether it's a dream, or merely a wonderful Christmas, which is pretty much the same thing," Pooh murmured happily to himself, "I hope neither one ends before I've eaten!"

Then the realization descended on the suddenly over-awed little bear of what was an even more wonderful present than a pantry full of everything he'd asked for. What better way to celebrate Christmas than with a memory, even the memory of a dream, of helping someone like Santa Claus, who spent all his time helping others?

"What a special present," exclaimed Pooh as his tummy filled with a warm feeling and his heart beat just a bit faster. "Because a happy memory, or a good dream, NEVER wears out . . . or needs to be filled up again!"

Pooh could hardly wait to tell his friends. As soon as he got dressed, he decided, he was going to go visit every one of his neighbors in the Hundred-Acre Wood and regale them with his adventure!

Then, the overflowing pantry caught Pooh Bear's eye.

"Well," he said to himself with a chuckle, "right after breakfast!"

"Pooh Bear," asked Christopher Robin as their walk through the Hundred-Acre Wood continued, "why are you smacking your lips?"

Pooh looked around, startled, and realized he'd only been remembering, and that breakfast was a long, long time ago.

"Oh," answered the disappointed but ever hopeful Pooh, "I was just thinking . . . we wouldn't happen to be on our way to breakfast . . . would we?"

"Silly old bear," laughed Christopher Robin. "We're not here for breakfast. We're here to sing carols."

"Sing Carol's what?" asked the totally confused bear.

"Christmas carols," responded Christopher Robin.

"I don't believe I know her," said Pooh, straining to remember.

"Carols are not a person, Pooh," Christopher Robin said slowly. "They're songs. Songs we sing on Christmas."

"Oh," said Pooh Bear. "And what do we sing when Carol's not here?"

Christopher Robin put his arm around his best friend's shoulder. "Don't worry, Pooh," he said, smiling affectionately at the bear. "I'll explain it when all the others are here."

"Good," sighed a relieved Pooh. He liked Christopher Robin's explanations even if he couldn't always remember them. They were like light in a dark room. And, as everyone knew, light and Christmas were the closest of friends.

"Along with Carol," Pooh murmured happily to himself.

A Very Small Christmas

Piglet loved *almost* everything about the night before Christmas. There was, for instance, the beautifully decorated Christmas tree that needn't be very tall or very wide. It could actually be a very small tree that suited the very small Piglet very well indeed (even if the tippity-top was still out of reach).

And there were all the unopened presents spread out beneath the tree and hidden about the house: stashed under the bed, tucked away in the back of the underwear drawer, and nestled safely out of reach atop the shelves of the linen closet. Piglet so appreciated the looks of an artistically papered and beribboned present that he often wrapped and bowed empty boxes simply because of the Christmassy feeling they gave his home. And, later, amid all the unwrapping (during which he was ever so careful not to tear the paper so it could be used again next year), he was occasionally

surprised by a gift with which he'd treated himself and then forgotten all about! Piglet's very small memory was another thing he loved about Christmas.

But the aspect of Christmas Eve that Piglet cherished most was the candles! Candles alight everywhere, flickering as decorations on the tree and lined up smartly across the mantel (right above his freshly starched and pressed—and very small—Christmas stocking), arranged according to size with a tall, thin candle on one end and a short, squat one on the other, all glowing cozily.

On a table next to his upholstered armchair (which had a ruffle around the bottom) sat another candle, as thick as a barber pole and sporting the same red, white, and blue stripes and topped by a bright yellow flame.

There were candles in the kitchen, candles in the corridor, candles in the bedroom, and candles in the bath. With so many candles burning all at once, Piglet was especially careful to make certain that no accidents happened to his candles, to himself, or to his very small but brightly illuminated home.

The warm, waxy glimmerings so pleased Piglet that he always waited until the last moment to kindle a fire in the fireplace so as not to spoil too soon the flickering candle lights playing across the walls and ceilings. It made him feel safe and serene and cared for, which helped him not to think about the one thing Piglet did *not* like about the night before Christmas. It was the same thing he didn't like about any night. They were all so very, VERY dark!

"You never realize," Piglet sighed to himself in a tiny voice, "how short a day is until you're afraid of the dark."

Piglet's consolation was that this Christmas he'd asked Santa to bring him a night-light to keep him company on all the dark nights to come. In the meantime, his candles would provide him with companionship until, just before he fell asleep, he would carefully extinguish every one (candles needed their rest, too) and toss and turn restlessly on the edge of sleep for the remainder of the dark, candleless night while Santa delivered his gifts.

A yawn suddenly widened Piglet's very small mouth into a round, sleepy O and he stretched contentedly in the warm glow of his candles. Yawns never bothered Piglet. And, although he always covered his mouth politely when they made themselves known, he was glad when they came.

"A yawn," he chuckled to himself, "is simply a smile caught with its mouth open."

Suddenly, a small scratching sounded outside his snugly locked and bolted front door!

Piglet dived for cover! When he found himself safely out of sight beneath his favorite upholstered armchair (with the ruffle around the bottom), he told himself in as reassuring a voice as such a very small animal could manage, "Perhaps it was simply the wind," which was a very real possibility because it was quite a blustery Christmas Eve.

He wasn't reassured for long, however. The scratching sounded again in a most insistent—and very unwindlike—manner!

Piglet breathed a deep, gulping sigh of woe.

"I suppose," he murmured, "that I should go see who . . . ," he paused to gulp nervously, ". . . or WHAT it is!" A small start and squeak of surprise escaped him when the scratching came again, as if agreeing that this was a very good idea, indeed!

As Piglet crawled out from under the upholstered armchair (with the ruffle around the bottom), an idea occurred to him.

"I don't have to open the door to see," he told himself with relief. "I can simply take a very small peek out of the window."

Pushing a stool up to the windowsill just off to one side of his front door, Piglet clambered atop it and cautiously peered out through the glass. The door, however, was too much to one side for him to see clearly no matter how he flattened his nose against the icy cold windowpanes.

"I suppose," he breathed softly to himself, "it wouldn't hurt to open the window just a very small smidgen of an opening."

But as soon as Piglet slid open the window just the tiniest bit, a huge gust of wind chose that moment to blast through the crack and see what Christmas Eve was like on the *inside* of a house!

Now, as is well known, gently flickering candle flames and rough gusts of rambunctious breeze are not the most amiable of acquaintances.

In no time at all, the mischievous breeze blew through the living room, wafted around the kitchen, bustled into the bedroom, and blasted out of the bath to exit out the window Piglet was too surprised to close until the damage had been done. Every candle in Piglet's house had been extinguished and, if it were possible, it was now darker inside than out in the night of moaning wind.

"At least," the frightened Piglet stammered to himself, "I certainly *hope* it's the wind that's moaning."

Suddenly, the scratching sounded once again and, to Piglet's great surprise, he noticed a small, fluttering light—not inside his house but emerging dimly, then brightly, then dimly again through the crack beneath his securely fastened front door!

Oh my! thought Piglet. If all the light is on the outside, then I'd be very foolish not to open the door and let it in!

Without hesitating another moment, the very small—but

oh-so-very-brave—animal unlocked, unbolted, and threw open the heavy portal, letting in the billowing night!

Darkness, however, was not what the wind blew into Piglet's house this time, but a small flickering light, caught in the breeze's grip and swirling and spinning out of control about the living-room ceiling! Desperately trying to escape the clutches of the rowdy breeze, the flickering spot of light managed to grab hold and cling to the tip-top of Piglet's Christmas tree, where it swayed back and forth, glimmering determinedly while the wind tried in vain to loosen its grip.

Piglet, frozen in awe at the still-open door, watched the struggle in openmouthed wonder. That very high (even on his very small tree), very pointy part had always been a great disappointment to him because he could never reach high enough to decorate it properly. And now this mysterious light had arrived under such strange circumstances and made his tree

more like Christmas than he'd ever thought possible!

It took a moment for Piglet to recover from his amazement at the light's presence and slam the front door shut. As soon as the door began to close, of course, the pesky wind darted back outside where it felt most at home, leaving Piglet alone with the light twittering vigorously atop the Christmas tree, as though trying to regain its breath after the long struggle with the vexing breeze.

Piglet, now that his home was illuminated by the eerie

yet warmly appealing light, was hesitant to relight his candles and spoil the marvelous show, almost like a display of tiny fireworks. He held out a plate of cookies cut into Christmas shapes toward the light.

"Would you care for some refreshment?" Piglet asked politely. "You're very welcome here. In fact," Piglet continued, trying not to blush with embarrassment, "I'm very glad you came."

As if in response, the light drifted down and settled gossamerlike at the tip of a Christmas-tree-shaped cookie. Now Piglet could see that it wasn't just a light, but a tiny firefly. He couldn't tell if the insect was actually eating the cookie, but its light seemed to grow stronger, as if simply being close

to a friendly someone was all the nourishment it needed. Piglet smiled. He knew that feeling well. It was one of his favorites.

"It seems," Piglet suggested, making polite conversation, "that you've been surprised by the arrival of winter."

The lightning bug shimmered his agreement.

"Well," smiled Piglet, "you're quite welcome to stay as long as you like."

He picked up a candle in its holder, intending to light his way to bed with it as soon as he found a match.

"It's long past my bedtime," explained Piglet to the glowing firefly, "so, if you'll excuse me, I must be off to sleep."

Before he could leave, however, the firefly fluttered up and perched on the cold wick of the unlit candle in Piglet's hand, blinking a question.

"Why, of course you may come with me," responded Piglet.

And so Piglet had the very best night's sleep, Christmas Eve or otherwise, that he'd ever had, with his houseguest twinkling merrily on his bedpost to the accompaniment of some very small snores.

The next morning, *Christmas* morning, Piglet and the firefly were up with the sun, going through the presents stuffed in his stocking. As Piglet reached the bottom, however, a look of consternation weighed his face into a frown.

"Oh dear," he sighed. "Santa forgot to give me my night-light. And that's what I wanted the most."

The bug sparkled sympathetically.

"He forgot your present, too?" asked Piglet in surprise. "What did you ask him for?

"A home out of the winter wind," murmured Piglet, reading the bug's glinting response.

Suddenly, like the sun rising and chasing off a night full of bad dreams, a thought occurred to Piglet.

"You don't suppose . . . ," he began, hardly able to believe such a wonderful idea. "You don't suppose that Santa

was making this our best Christmas ever by bringing us together . . . do you?"

The firefly blinked what seemed to Piglet's eyes to be a bright affirmation.

"It simply goes to show," remarked Piglet that night to the firefly as he sat glowing contentedly on the bedpost, "that sometimes the very small things at Christmas are the very best things."

And the firefly twinkled his agreement.

"Singin' Christmas songs is one o' the things Tiggers do best," hooted the striped and bouncing feline to his gathered neighbors. He stood in a group that included Rabbit, Gopher, Eeyore, Piglet, Kanga, and little Roo, all facing Christopher Robin and Pooh Bear. "And one of the things Carol does best, too," Pooh assured everyone.

Everyone exchanged a puzzled look.

"Carol?" sniffed Rabbit. "Who is Carol?"

"And why isn't she here if she's going to sing with us?" rumbled Eeyore. "If no one minds my asking."

"There is no Carol," Christopher Robin began to explain.

"But you said she was going to be here," whistled Gopher.

"And why is her first name Christmas?" Roo wanted to know.

"If you'll all be a little patient, I'll tell you everything," sighed Christopher Robin. "It seems Pooh is stuck on a certain idea and, with all of your help, we'll unstick him."

Everyone nodded and murmured in sudden understanding. An idea stuck in Pooh Bear's head was a very common happenstance. Christmas was as good a day as any for that to occur.

Pooh smiled back at them and nodded. He remembered that ideas weren't the only things one could get stuck in on Christmas.

Stuck on Christmas

Christmas was Rabbit's favorite time of year. It was, of course, everyone else's favorite, too, but Rabbit, who always managed to create a spectacular event out of the smallest occasion, inevitably tumbled lop-ears over cottontail when it came to Christmas. There was simply no ignoring ol' long ears' pre-Christmas frenzy. Everything had to be perfect . . . *more* than perfect, if that were possible, and when it came to Rabbit and Christmas, NOTHING was impossible!

On the day before Christmas, Rabbit would produce a large scrap of paper, which had seen almost as many Christmases as Rabbit himself, entitled "Christmas List or Things That Need to Be Done, Undone, Done Over, or Overdone Before Christmas, Written by Me!"

And, on the bottom of the paper, right under "Me," he'd written "Rabbit" in his very best handwriting. This wasn't because Rabbit didn't know who "Me" was. He recognized his own handwriting. But everyone knew that a list, which was any sort of list at all, simply must have a name written on the bottom in very neat handwriting.

"And why not mine?" Rabbit whispered to himself

proudly, as he did every year when he brought out the list. "It's my list after all."

"Now, let me see . . . ," mused Rabbit, reading carefully. "Dirt banished, grime expelled, and dust bunnies on the run. Check!"

Rabbit made a huge check mark in the appropriate place on the page with his pencil. Then he read the next item.

"Goodies prepared, tasted . . . ," he smacked his lips happily at the remembrance of this task, "and packed into Christmas presents for anyone with the good taste to think my treats taste good . . . which is everyone!" He made another self-satisfied check.

"Tree potted and ornamented," he continued, making another check mark as he smugly surveyed the meticulous decorations on the tree tucked comfortably in a corner.

"Doodads looking dandy," Rabbit confirmed, surveying the ceramic carrot candleholders on the mantel, where candles were kept burning all of Christmas night so Santa

wouldn't have any trouble finding the stocking to stuff full of presents. And, sitting regally in its place of honor, was the Santa-shaped squash plucked from a past harvest. Rabbit was certain it was a *smiling* Santa squash, although no one else could detect a mouth on the vegetable, let alone a smile.

"Check!" Rabbit announced and made another mark on his list.

He wriggled his toes in satisfaction, filling the room with the sound of miniature chimes. For Christmas also marked the appearance of Rabbit's reindeer slippers with tiny bells sewn onto the tips of their antlers, which jingled merrily as Rabbit scurried about his Christmas business, his feet warm and comfy.

Rabbit, confident that everything was now placed just so for Christmas, took one last look at his list. And there, on the bottom of the paper, conspicuously without a check mark, he read, "Sweep the chimney." At that instant, a vigorous and unhappy sneeze came roaring out of Rabbit's nose!

"ACHOO!

"Soot!" he sniffed in disgust as he tenderly pinched his nose to make sure it hadn't been sneezed loose. Just the thought of all that insidious black gunk hiding up the chimney made his nose tickle until it couldn't stand it anymore and had to explode in a nostril-clearing sneeze!

Rabbit dreaded it from the tops of his floppy ears to the tips of his reindeer-covered toenails, but the year's accumulation of soot had to be swept out of the chimney before he could bear to think about Santa Claus sliding down it.

In no time, Rabbit had donned his baggy coveralls,

carefully pulled a clean white stocking over each ear, strapped on a pair of goggles, and tied a starched bandanna over his nose and mouth. Sweeping a chimney was no time to have soot playing hide-and-seek up such a sensitive nose.

Then he marched to the hall closet, pulled out the circular soot brush with the hard, stiff bristles, and attached it to the longest handle he could find.

He was ready!

Rabbit quickly marched to the hearth—which had been carefully swept out and covered with a drop cloth in anticipation—and craned his neck for a look up the dark chimney. High above, a small patch of blue sky could be seen through the hole where the smoke escaped.

"Humph," sniffed rabbit. "Worse than I thought."

Applying his brush liberally, it didn't take him long to

scrub the chimney clean as far up as his brush could reach. Unfortunately, it couldn't reach all the way to the top.

"Oh well," sighed Rabbit, giving his tail a quick wiggle to shake off the fallen soot, "there's more than one way to scrub a chimney."

It was hardly any time at all before Rabbit was up on the roof looking down where he'd been looking up just the moment before.

"Now I've got you!" he chuckled triumphantly and set to work.

But the handle was not quite long enough from this direction either. As a result, the bottom part of the chimney was neatly swept, and the top was scoured spick-and-span, but the section in the middle was unbrushed and—if it was possible for soot to smirk—that's what it was doing to the frustrated Rabbit.

But Rabbit was not about to let a handful of soot—smirking or otherwise—get the best of him.

Standing on the very tips of the toes of his reindeer slippers, tongue tucked tightly into the corner of his mouth in rapt concentration, Rabbit leaned down into the chimney as far as he could stretch. . . .

All of a sudden, his feet slipped out from under him and, with a helpless squawk of distress, he plunged headfirst down the chimney!

To Rabbit's great relief, he didn't tumble very far. It seemed all the diligent tasting he'd done earlier had increased the size of his middle just enough so that the last place his tummy was going to go was down a narrow chimney.

So there he was, upside down and stuck half in and half out of the chimney, his feet emerging from the top of the smoke hole and kicking wildly, and the bells on his reindeer slippers tinkling anxiously.

"Help!" yelled Rabbit, his voice echoing hollowly down the chimney. "Heellllppp!"

At that particular moment, Winnie the Pooh and his very good friend Piglet were walking up the path toward Rabbit's house, their arms laden with seasonal treats and presents to be delivered to Rabbit.

"Help!" boomed Rabbit's voice once again, stopping the startled Pooh Bear and Piglet right in their tracks.

"What . . . what was THAT?" squeaked Piglet as he scurried behind Pooh for protection.

"I believe," replied Pooh, looking up thoughtfully, "it's that person standing in Rabbit's chimney waving those reindeer mittens at us."

Piglet peered cautiously out from behind Pooh for a look.

"Oh dear!" uttered Piglet with a small gasp. "Rabbit's stuck upside down in his chimney!"

"Upside down?" responded Pooh, taking a closer look. "It looks like his downside is up, to me."

"I think that's the same thing, Pooh," suggested Piglet.

"Poor Rabbit," moaned Pooh. "They both appear to have happened to him at the same time . . . haven't they? His upside downing and all that?"

Piglet and Pooh hurried to Rabbit's fireplace and looked up the chimney. It was impossible to see anything because the stuck Rabbit was preventing any light from shining down into the chimney.

"Don't worry, Rabbit," called Pooh reassuringly. "I'll be right up!"

"Stop!" yelled Rabbit. "Don't come up, Pooh! Get me down!"

Pooh Bear scratched his head thoughtfully.

"Don't I have to go up first . . . ," he asked Piglet, "to come down . . . last?"

"I don't know, Pooh," answered Piglet with a mournful shrug.

"Good," smiled Pooh. "I always have my best ideas when I don't know what I'm doing."

Without a moment's delay, Pooh shoved himself up the chimney and began to climb. Despite a great deal of wheezing and not a few grunts, Pooh didn't make much progress past his own ample middle. Piglet watched Pooh's kicking and scrambling feet hopefully, but they proceeded no further up the chimney.

"Ah," came Pooh's voice, "I seem to be stuck."

"Why, Pooh! The chimney's too tight!" Piglet called up to him. "You've found the problem!"

"I have?" Pooh answered in delighted surprise.

"Wonderful," sniffed the exasperated Rabbit. "Now what?"

"Well," responded Pooh, "since I've found the problem, do you suppose we could ask someone else to find the solution?"

The word was sent out and soon Tigger, Eeyore, and Gopher were standing with Piglet, looking at Pooh's legs dangling from the chimney.

"I say we blassst," asserted Gopher after a thorough examination. "Couple o' sssticks o' dynamite ought to do the trick."

"Oh my goodness," Rabbit's voice wailed down the chimney.

"If you don't mind my saying," rumbled Eeyore, "I don't think you want to do that."

"Why not?" demanded Gopher.

"Because we don't want to hurt Rabbit's chimney," suggested Pooh hopefully, "it being Christmas Eve and Santa needing it to slide down and all."

"Guess that makes sssense," mumbled the disappointed Gopher.

"Thank goodness," sighed Rabbit.

"This is a pretty tall problem," mumbled Gopher, scratching his head under his mining helmet.

"I'll say," laughed Tigger. "At least four feet." He pointed to Pooh's feet protruding from the chimney. "There's two of 'em now! Hoo-hoo-*hoo*!"

"Perhaps," suggested Piglet, wringing his hands nervously, "if we figured out what comes out of a chimney, we could include Pooh and Rabbit somehow?"

"Yeah!" laughed Tigger. "Figuring things out is what Tiggers do best!"

"What comes OUT of a chimney?" Gopher carefully considered this question while he scratched his chin thoughtfully.

"Smoke," suggested Eeyore.

"Soot!" shouted Rabbit.

"Santa?" Pooh asked hopefully.

"Sssmoke, sssoot, and Sssanta," whistled Gopher. "Sssounds like we're on to sssomethin' to me."

"It's s's!" hooted Tigger. "S's come out of chimneys!"

"How does that help Rabbit and Pooh?" Eeyore spoke up. "If no one minds my asking."

"I don't know," sighed Piglet.

"Pooh and Rabbit," barked Gopher, smacking his fist into his palm, "need to come sssslippin' and sssslidin' out of the chimney like . . . like . . ." He struggled to complete his thought.

Rabbit, who had been listening to this conversation so intently that he hadn't noticed that the handkerchief over his nose had slipped, suddenly found himself with a noseful of soot and unexpectedly produced a mighty sneeze!

"ACHOOOOOOOOO!"

The force of the explosion popped Pooh out of the chimney and left him sitting thoughtfully in the fireplace.

"Like a sssneeze out of a nossse?" Pooh suggested hopefully to his startled friends.

There was a shocked silence. Then everyone except Rabbit, who wasn't at all certain of what was taking place, shouted in unison, "Sssneezes!"

Rabbit responded with a hesitant "Bless you?" which no one seemed to notice.

"All we need is a little sssseasoning," laughed Gopher.

Before Pooh or Rabbit could ask any questions, Gopher was standing in the fireplace holding a handful of pepper while Tigger stood prepared to blast it up the chimney with a pair of hand bellows.

"Let 'er rip," Gopher ordered Tigger as he held his nose with his free hand.

Tigger squeezed the bellows and, with a loud wheeze, a stream of air dispersed the pepper up into the chimney!

Barely any time had elapsed before Rabbit emitted the biggest sneeze of all!

"ACHOOOOOOOOOOOOO!"

This explosion blew Rabbit up and out of the chimney, spun him about in midair, and dropped him back down into the chimney so hard that not even Pooh's middle, let alone Rabbit's, would have stopped his descent this time!

"Yeeiiaaa!" squealed Rabbit as he plunged down the dark chimney, completely clearing it of soot!

Pooh, wanting to make quite certain that all was going according to plan—he didn't recall exactly what the plan was, but he knew there was one—picked that instant to look up the chimney. It was just in time! Rabbit made a soft landing on his furry friend in a shower of the remaining soot.

"Achoo!" said Rabbit.

"You're very welcome," replied his friends.

Later, after all the spilled soot had been swept far, FAR away, the friends sat before a cozy fire in the spotless hearth, sipping mugs of cocoa and waiting for the sleep that comes before the arrival of Santa and Christmas morning. Rabbit sighed contentedly.

"It will be wonderful to see what Santa brings, but I think I've already had the very best Christmas present I could have."

"A clean chimney?" Piglet guessed.

"No," smiled Rabbit, "the help of my very best friends in solving quite an embarrassing problem."

"Aw, don't be embarrassed, bunny boy," said Tigger reassuringly. "That's what friends are for!"

"And what Christmas is for, too," added Eeyore, "when you get right down to it."

"That's right," chuckled Pooh. "There are so many very nice things about Christmas that it's a holiday difficult *not* to be stuck on, one way or another."

Rabbit smiled wryly and put his arm around the bear of little brain. "Thank you, Pooh Bear. Merry Christmas."

"Merry Christmas, Rabbit," responded Pooh happily.

"And we go from house to house and sing these Christmas songs," Christopher Robin looked pointedly at Pooh (who was trying very hard to listen and remember), "called carols, to help everyone enjoy the fact that it's Christmas Eve."

"But won't our houses be empty?" pointed out Piglet in a very small voice. "We'll all be out here singing."

"A house likes a nice song as well as anyone else," Eeyore murmured in his low voice.

"As long as we don't sing too high," he added with a sad shake of his mane.

"Why not sing high to a house?" Christopher Robin whispered to Pooh.

"Because," Pooh whispered back, "if we sing too *high* to Eeyore's house, it won't be long until it's too *low* to live in anymore."

And Pooh, in a very *low* voice, went on to tell Christopher Robin about a certain *unstable* Christmas Eve.

Unstable Christmas

Eeyore was feeling awfully grumpy. But for Eeyore, of course, feeling awfully grumpy meant that he was actually feeling remarkably happy. It had been a splendid day. His tail had fallen off only once, the thistles he'd had for breakfast had just the proper amount of snap and crackle, *and* it was the night before Christmas! And coming in third (behind tails and thistles) meant Christmas Eve held a very special place in Eeyore's heart, although he wouldn't want anyone going out of his way to notice such a thing.

"Folks have enough to do," rumbled Eeyore, "without havin' to worry about yours truly."

The thing that made Christmas Eve significant to Eeyore was the excuse that it gave him to fix up his dilapidated dwelling of sticks and logs without attracting a lot of fuss and questions from his neighbors. The lean-to's run-down (and often quite precarious) state didn't usually claim the attention of the laid-back donkey, but every year the spirit of Christmas urged the usually hesitant Eeyore to throw himself into some seasonal decorating.

"There's somethin' about a stable this time o' year," Eeyore would tell himself thoughtfully, "that makes you want to do something special."

He heaved a long sigh. "Even if no one notices but me."

But others *did* notice. It was impossible not to, because Eeyore's house had never looked more beautiful!

The first item to catch a passerby's eye was the splendid green wreath hanging over the entrance. Woven among the tenderly intertwined green sprigs of the wreath were lengths of candy-apple red and snow white ribbons.

Next, carefully hung upon the house's sparse framework were clusters of brightly colored cranberries, highlighting the house in the same way ornaments illuminate a Christmas tree.

Then there were the long evergreen streamers, dotted

with frosted pinecones and draped strategically to cover all the pesky holes in Eeyore's roof of sticks.

"Magnificent," breathed Rabbit in wonder when he happened by and noticed the transformation. "It's as pretty as a garden of freshly sprouted vegetables."

"Oh my, Eeyore," chuckled the delighted Pooh at his first sight of the decorations. "It looks good enough to *eat*!" And the bear's tummy growled a small grumble to show that he meant it.

Tigger was so impressed when he noticed Eeyore's house that he stopped practically in midbounce and came out with the highest compliment he could think of.

"If it had strip-e-dies, it'd be purr-fect," he purred. And added an enthusiastic "Hoo-hoo-*hoo*!" because it was simply too exciting not to.

Piglet gave himself a hug of happiness when he first saw the house and blurted out (but in a very small voice), "I don't think I've ever seen your house holding together quite so very nicely! What a wonderful place to spend Christmas!"

Gopher, of course, whistled a long, low, and very impressed whistle. "Looksss as warm and cozy as a tunnel in a ssssnowsssstorm," he sniffed.

Eeyore, being Eeyore, tried not to show it, but in fact he was very pleased.

"Thanks," he rumbled, lowering his head shyly so his friends wouldn't see his happy grin, "but I know you all are just sayin' that to be nice."

"I think we're all saying it," contradicted Pooh with a smile as he gave the donkey a warm pat on the back, "because it *is* nice, Eeyore. Just like you."

Needless to say, Eeyore was feeling that this particular Christmas Eve was going to be the very best night before Christmas he could remember. There was only one little thing left to do; then the donkey would be able to just sit back on his tail (careful not to push too hard on its very sharp pin, of course) and enjoy the magical evening.

But this one final thing left to be done was, with no perhaps about it, the very most important task to be carried out on Christmas Eve. Eeyore had to hang up his stocking so that Santa would have no trouble finding it. And, to make certain the search was even less of a strain on this, the busiest night of Santa's year, Eeyore chose a long stocking of yellow yarn so bright that it almost glowed in the dark. This stocking also possessed an extra large toe to allow ample space for all the presents Eeyore was wishing for.

Barely able to contain his excitement, Eeyore took a tack into his mouth and gently pushed it into the front stick until it stayed by itself, hanging precariously by its tip.

"Now," declared Eeyore, picking up a hammer, "one little tap and I can have my stocking up and be all ready for Christmas!"

Eeyore gave the tack a sharp rap with the hammer. Then he draped his colorful stocking on it and smiled contentedly at the sight it made.

But then a tiny creaking from his wall of sticks replaced the smile on Eeyore's face with a frown. And when this was followed almost immediately by a groaning rumble from the roof, the donkey knew it was time to beat a hasty exit!

Eeyore had no sooner galloped out his front door than

the creaking and groaning combined into an earsplitting roar as the house of sticks and twigs collapsed, almost snatching off the fleeing Eeyore's tail. When the swirling dust finally settled, all that remained of Eeyore's house was something that strongly resembled a pile of firewood nicely decorated for Christmas.

All of Eeyore's neighbors heard the awesome crash and knew precisely what it meant. They'd heard it many times before. But as they hurried to make certain that Eeyore was

not hurt, they hoped against hope that, perhaps this time, it was something else that had fallen down. Perhaps this time the structure their friend had labored so mightily to construct in order to welcome Christmas properly was safe and sound and still standing.

When they arrived from every direction of the Hundred-Acre Wood, however, their hearts drooped along with the corners of their mouths. Standing in the midst of what had once been his stable stood Eeyore, extracting from the mess his stocking, which still glowed brightly, its yellow color undiminished by the mishap.

"Oh dear," mourned Piglet, sniffing back a tear. No one else needed to speak. They all felt exactly the same and were struggling to hold back tears of their own.

"I suppose," rumbled Eeyore, trying to put on a brave face, "I'll have to find someplace else to hang my Christmas stocking this year."

"Oh, I don't think so, Eeyore," exclaimed Pooh. "It will look so nice in your house."

"Pooh Bear," protested Rabbit in a fierce whisper, "he doesn't have a house anymore."

"Certainly he does, Rabbit," laughed Pooh as he pointed to the pile of sticks and twigs. "There it is! It simply needs a bit of . . . untangling."

"Buddy bear's right," hooted Tigger. "And we're just the bunch to untangle it, too!"

"But it's already Christmas Eve," pointed out Eeyore with his sadly sagging chin nearly touching the ground. "We'll never get it ready in time for Santa to find my stocking!"

"Not if we don't get a move on!" declared Gopher, excited by the idea of rebuilding Eeyore's house.

Eeyore hung his stocking out of the way on the branch of a nearby tree and everyone set to work.

Rabbit immediately took on the task of supervising the reconstruction. He was always happiest giving orders, and it didn't matter in the least whether anyone followed them or not as long as *he* could be in charge. And since the work always got done no matter what Rabbit said, no one really minded.

Gopher immediately began excavating neat holes in which the posts supporting the new house would be set.

In the meantime, Pooh was performing a careful search of the area surrounding the past and future house.

"For Eeyore's house to have looked good enough to eat," Pooh Bear told himself thoughtfully, "something tasty is now missing. And I'm just the bear to find it."

Eeyore carefully separated the twigs and logs and other stuff into piles. One pile was for the roof, another for the walls, and one last one for all those items that no one was sure what they were good for but were too important-looking to throw away.

Pooh tromped around and around in the snow, looking beneath rocks (the sort that could be lifted without much effort) and above bushes (which only required a minimum of tip-top-toeing), but he still hadn't found what he was looking for.

"Whatever that is," he sighed.

Once all the debris had been carefully set aside, Piglet meticulously swept the foundation.

"Being neat as a pin lets happiness in," he rhymed neatly

as he vigorously plied his broom. "And a house, old or new, has room for happiness, too!"

Tigger was bouncing vigorously about, collecting only the thickest evergreen boughs from the tippety-top of the trees.

"The fuzzier the roof," he chuckled, "the warmer the house."

Pooh watched in wonder. All the activity made him decide to stop his search for whatever it was for a moment and sit down. The bear of little brain had learned long ago that the best way to keep from being lazy was to take a rest *before* he got tired!

"YIKES!" Pooh squeaked and stood up quite suddenly, rubbing his sitter-downer.

"Thank you, Pooh Bear," said a grateful Eeyore. "I was looking for those thistles. They're my Christmas dinner."

"You're very welcome, Eeyore," responded Pooh, rubbing his bottom thoughtfully. "I was certain there was something tasty around here that needed finding. But I am surprised at what I found it with!"

Everyone continued to work frantically to get Eeyore's house rebuilt and decorated so he could hang his stocking in time for Santa's arrival.

However, despite everyone's best efforts, the rebuilding was not completed until the sun was well up Christmas morning.

"I'm sorry, Eeyore," apologized the exhausted Rabbit. "I suppose you missed Santa."

All the donkey's weary friends added their sympathy.

Eeyore smiled his thanks. "Stop feeling so gloomy," he told them. "I may have missed a few presents, but friends are what make a house a home. This holiday may only come once a year, but you all make it Christmas *every* day!"

"You certainly are a good loser, Eeyore," remarked Tigger admiringly.

"Well," shrugged the donkey modestly, "being a good loser means you always have somebody who likes to play with you."

"C'mon, Eeyore," appealed Piglet. "Let's see how your stocking looks hanging in your new house. Who cares if it's empty!"

"All right," agreed Eeyore. "Then I can fix you all something to eat."

"What a good idea," laughed Pooh, patting his growling tummy. "Just as long as we don't have to sit on it," he added cautiously.

What they didn't find hanging from the tree, however, was an EMPTY stocking. It was so full, in fact, that it looked like a giant banana ready to burst out of its skin! As his friends looked on in wonder, Eeyore spilled the stocking's contents out onto the ground, and they all discovered that there were presents for each and every one of them!

"Well, I'll be," breathed the flabbergasted Gopher.

"Be what?" asked Tigger.

"Grateful that it's Christmas," responded Rabbit, shaking his head in awe.

Eeyore surveyed the presents thoughtfully as a small smile spread itself over his face.

"I suppose," he said slowly, "that as long as Christmas is made welcome, it will find you no matter what."

"Yes," chuckled Pooh Bear. "Rather like a thistle, only with a much happier ENDING!"

"Are we only going to sing to houses?" Roo demanded of Christopher Robin.

"Well," laughed Christopher Robin, "who else do you suggest?"

"The snow people," breathed Roo in wonder, black eyes sparkling.

"Snow people?" responded Christopher Robin in surprise. He looked around at the others questioningly. They all looked at one another and put their fingers to their lips.

As Roo bounced off to look for snow people to sing to, Kanga hopped up next to Christopher Robin and, with a chuckle, began to whisper a story into his ear.

Snow Time like Christmas

"But, Mama," moaned the distressed Roo, "how can it be Christmas Eve when there's no snow?"

"It is strange," sighed Kanga. "I've never known the Hundred-Acre Wood not to have snow by Christmas."

Kanga and little Roo were looking forlornly out of their open front door at the barren forest. The leaves had all departed long ago and the carpets of grass had exchanged their crisp green color for somber browns, like children trading their colorful play clothes for warm pajamas to wear through the long winter's sleep.

"You think the snow will ever come, Mama?" Roo asked anxiously. "It just doesn't seem like Christmas at *all*!"

"I don't know, Roo dear," answered Kanga with a shrug. "Snow, like all weather, has a mind of its own."

Then Kanga smiled down at the woeful expression on her son's face.

"Don't worry, Roo," she told him with a reassuring pat

on the head. "Just because the snow is silly enough to miss Christmas doesn't mean we have to."

"Yeah!" agreed Roo with a laugh. "An' if it's really the night before Christmas, I have some presents to deliver!"

"Whatever do you mean?" the surprised Kanga wanted to know.

"Well, you see," began Roo, hopping nervously from one foot to the other as he tried to explain, "I thought it wasn't going to be Christmas 'til it snowed and that I had plenty o' time so I haven't delivered any of the presents I've gotten for our friends! See?"

Kanga shook her head in exasperated amusement. "Oh dear," she sighed. "It's a good thing you didn't wait any longer. I suppose I'll have to—"

"Can I deliver them now, Mama?" interrupted Roo excitedly.

Kanga glanced outside and her brows knitted together into a mother's worried expression.

"It's going to be dark very soon," she began slowly.

Roo, jumping up and down in his excitement, couldn't wait for her to finish.

"I won't get lost, Mama," he protested. "I just *have* to deliver my presents on time! I don't want anyone to think I forgot them on Christmas."

"All right, Roo," answered Kanga with a smile. Then she held up a warning finger. "But promise to stay on the path and come straight home when you're finished."

"Okay, Mama," piped Roo happily in response. "I promise."

Just a very few minutes later, Roo was hopping rapidly

down the path with a sackful of presents for his friends slung over his shoulder.

Then, something cold and wet burst on the tip of Roo's small pointed nose. Before his startled gaze drifted *another* snowflake with—as is the case of most snowflakes—a great many more right behind it!

"Hurray!" squeaked the delighted Roo. "You made it in time for Christmas and I'm very glad to see you." He grinned and lifted his face to the falling snow. "And I'm sure everyone else will be, too," he laughed and poked out his tongue to catch the falling frozen drops of wetness.

And at that very moment, the other inhabitants of the Hundred-Acre Wood were indeed delighting in the descending snow, which grew more and more frenzied, as if all the snowflakes wanted to be on hand for the arrival of Christmas morning.

Winnie the Pooh stuck his head out of a window and chuckled as the thickly falling snowflakes seemed to vie with one another for the excitement of plunging down the neck of the bear's red jersey and tickling him into laughter.

From an upper-story window of Rabbit's house, ol' long ears greeted the faster and faster falling snow with a sniff of satisfaction. It was about time the garden got its annual blanket of white, he thought to himself. The only time it looked prettier was when it was sprouting the greens and reds and yellows and oranges of brightly colored vegetables.

Gopher's head emerged cautiously from the mouth of one of his numerous burrows and was instantly covered with a fine dusting of white snow, like frosting on a doughnut. He whistled, impressed by the amount of snow that was now tumbling from the sky. He smiled. A layer of snow on the ground always made his winter's sleep all the cozier. Gopher yawned in relaxed anticipation of the long nap to come.

Piglet was fiercely sweeping his walk, but the white curtain of winter was now descending much too quickly. As soon as he'd cleared one section of his front walk, another was buried in snow. With an exasperated sigh, Piglet leaned wearily on his broom and watched the snow gather in sparkling piles of white all over his walkway.

"Well," the very small animal told himself with a smile,

"at least it's very clean snow. It would be a pity if I had to wash it and pile it up myself." He giggled into his hand at such an idea and continued to observe the soft accumulation of white powder.

And Tigger was no sooner aware of the cascading snowflakes than he was out making snow Tiggers in the ice-cold fluff.

"'Cuz that's what Tiggers do best when it's snowifying," he laughed, then added a "Hoo-hoo-*hoo*!" for good measure.

Meanwhile, Eeyore watched the swirling, twirling, and wildly somersaulting snowflakes with a rueful smile.

"Well," he rumbled to himself, "at least the holes in my roof will have something to let inside the house. That'll make 'em happy."

And then the donkey smiled, because there was no one around to see it and because he was so fond of snow that he truly didn't mind it sharing his house with him.

Then, quite suddenly, on every face all over the Hundred-Acre Wood—from Pooh Bear to Eeyore—a realization popped open their eyes and mouths in amazement as they all thought the same thought at once!

"Oh my goodness," gasped Pooh.

"It's snowing . . . ," began Rabbit in thoughtful surprise.

". . . and that means . . . ," whistled the flabbergasted Gopher to himself.

". . . that it's almost Christmas," finished the suddenly very nervous Piglet.

"And Christmas means . . . ," gasped Tigger, rubbing his head in wonder.

"...that there are presents to be delivered," said Eeyore, "an' not much time to deliver 'em in!"

It wasn't very long at all before everyone was crisscrossing through the Hundred-Acre Wood, loaded down with presents that they left at one another's homes. By the time everything had been delivered, however, the snowstorm had turned into a blizzard, a whirling waterfall of white, falling so thickly and blowing so fiercely that it was impossible to tell whether there was a path underfoot or a tree in front of a nose. As a result, there were quite a number of misplaced paths, bumped trees, and bruised noses by the time all the presents had been properly placed.

In fact, the only one who wasn't having any trouble finding his way home in the blowing snow and falling darkness was little Roo. But then that wasn't so very unusual. Home

was where his Mama waited for him and nothing as minor as a howling blizzard can keep a child away from his mother.

But as he hopped along, each bounce jarring off the snow that tried to cling to him, Roo came across a strange sight. There was a snowman standing in the middle of what used to be the path before it was covered with snow, pondering in a very Pooh Bear sort of way.

"Hello," said Roo in surprise, shouting to be heard over the roar of the storm.

"Why, hello, Roo," the snowman shouted back, which surprised Roo even more because he could not recall ever hearing a snowman talk before, let alone call him by name. And he spoke in a voice that sounded very much like Pooh's!

"But that must be the storm playing tricks," Roo

decided. "Why else would a snowman sound like Winnie the Pooh?"

"I seem," shouted the snowman, "to be having a bit of bother finding my way home in this storm."

"Why don't you come home with me?" suggested Roo at the top of his voice.

"What a good idea," responded the snowman agreeably. "I suppose any home is a good home in the middle of a storm."

So Roo continued to hop toward home with the snowman stomping along behind on his short stubby legs.

But the evening's surprises were not over for Roo. Another snowman appeared out of the gloom, with long attachments on his head like feelers on a caterpillar. At Roo's invitation to join them, the second snowman, who was shivering so badly that he couldn't speak, nodded in happy acceptance. Roo found this very strange. "Who ever heard of a snowman who got too cold?" he asked himself.

"It must have something to do with Christmas Eve," Roo concluded. He was certain the magic of the holiday had to have something to do with these walking, talking, too-cold snow creatures.

The next snow being they came across had four legs and two heads! The second head appeared to be a very small animal with large pink ears sitting atop the first droopy-eared creature. Wow! thought the amazed Roo. Whoever made that snowman certainly had a lot of imagination!

The last snowperson who joined the procession to Roo's house carried another little snow creature in his arms that whistled when he talked. The voice sounded familiar, but Roo was getting tired and wanted to get home, so he didn't try very hard to figure out who he was reminded of.

And the snowman holding the whistler had a tail he kept sitting back on and was trying to hop like Roo. Roo was pleased to think that snowmen hopped, too, but this one wasn't very successful at hopping because of the snowman he was carrying in his arms.

When, at last, Roo saw the lights of his house shining brightly through the snow, he dashed ahead and flung open the door.

"Mama," he shouted. "I'm home just like I promised!"

Kanga ran out to meet him. "Good for you, dear," she smiled. Then she began brushing snow from her son. "You look almost like a snowman," she laughed.

"I brought home some company," Roo exclaimed, excitedly pointing to the snow creatures on the porch. "See?"

"How nice," responded Kanga. Much to her son's sur-

prise, she was not at all surprised by the sight of Roo's guests.

"I'll take care of our visitors," Kanga told Roo as she pushed him toward his bedroom, "while you get out of those wet clothes and put on some warm pajamas."

Roo was very anxious to ask the snow creatures about Christmas and magic and the best snow for snowballs, so he changed in no time at all.

But when he ran back into the parlor, the snowmen were gone! Sitting next to the fire, with pools of water puddling at their feet, were his friends Pooh, Rabbit, Piglet, Eeyore, Gopher, and Tigger, sipping mugs of hot chocolate in front of a cozy fire in Kanga's hearth.

"Where . . . ?" Roo sputtered, looking around in disappointment, "where are all the snowmen?"

"What snowmen, Roo dear?" asked Kanga with a quizzical look on her face.

"The ones who followed me home," he wailed. "The

magic ones that could walk and talk and shiver because it was Christmas Eve!"

"Oh," responded Rabbit, exchanging knowing looks with the others. "*Those* snowmen."

"Er . . . it was much too warm for them in here," blurted out Piglet nervously.

"Yeah," Tigger agreed. "They had to go back outside in the cold coolness."

"After all," Gopher whistled, "they have a lot to do and only one night a year to do it in."

"They were sorry they couldn't say good-bye," rumbled Eeyore.

"Oh bother," sighed Pooh sadly, "I'm sorry I missed them, too."

"Oh well," said Roo in a very disappointed voice. "At least I got to meet them."

"And there's always next year, Roo," sympathized Pooh, putting his arm around Roo's shoulders. "Perhaps I'll get to meet them then, too."

Kanga patted her son's head. "I'm certain they were glad to have met you, Roo dear."

"No doubt about *that*," sniffed Rabbit. "And just in the nick of time!"

"And they won't forget ya, kid," announced Tigger.

"They won't?" said Roo, brightening. "Are you sure?"

"As sure as my name is T-I–double Guh–Er!"

So, that night, after the snow had ceased falling and he'd said good night to everyone, Roo went to bed. He was very happy and dreamed good dreams about his new friends and hoped they had a wonderful Christmas Eve doing whatever it was snowmen did on Christmas Eve. But, most of all, he hoped he'd meet them again sometime.

And when Roo awoke Christmas morning, he not only discovered presents under his tree but also found a yard full of snowmen out the front door. Around them were the familiar footprints of his friends, circling, crossing, intersecting. Roo knew that there was no better place to spend Christmas than at his house. (And the snowmen, after a magical Christmas Eve, obviously knew it, too.) And that even if he never saw the walking and talking and shivering snowmen again, he'd never forget them.

And, after all, aren't good memories and magic what Christmas is all about?

"That was a wonderful way to spend a night before Christmas," sighed Pooh in contentment as he and Christopher Robin walked homeward through the snow. Everyone else had said good night and gone home to bed and to wait excitedly for Christmas morning.

"I like song singing," the bear continued happily, "especially when the words at the end of the lines all end with the same sound."

"That does make it pleasant," agreed Christopher Robin with a smile.

"But I do have one question, Christopher Robin," frowned Pooh, glancing up at his friend.

"And what is that, Pooh Bear?"

"Do I invite her to breakfast?" Pooh answered. "Or is she going to invite me?"

Christopher Robin, knowing the answer, tried not to laugh impolitely when he asked, "Whom do you mean, Pooh?"

"Why, Christmas Carol, of course," chuckled Pooh. "I'd very much like to meet her."

"Perhaps it will work out that you will someday, Pooh," responded Christopher Robin, placing his hand tenderly on his best friend's head.

"Good!" breathed Pooh happily. "Merry Christmas, Christopher Robin."

"Merry Christmas, silly old bear."